TRAPPED

TRAPPED

SIGMUND BROUWER

ORCA BOOK PUBLISHERS

Published in Canada and the United States
in 2022 by Orca Book Publishers.
orcabook.com

Library and Archives Canada Cataloguing in Publication
Title: Trapped / Sigmund Brouwer.
Names: Brouwer, Sigmund, 1959- author.
Description: Series statement: Orca anchor
Identifiers: Canadiana (print) 20210166541 |
Canadiana (ebook) 20210166606 | ISBN 9781459828612 (softcover) |
ISBN 9781459828629 (PDF) | ISBN 9781459828636 (EPUB)
Classification: LCC PS8553.R68467 T73 2022 | DDC jc813/.54—dc23

Library of Congress Control Number: 2021934072

Summary: In this high-interest accessible novel for teen readers, Matt
makes a startling discovery that he hides from his abusive foster parents.

Orca Book Publishers is committed to reducing the consumption
of nonrenewable resources in the production of our books. We make
every effort to use materials that support a sustainable future.

Orca Book Publishers gratefully acknowledges the support
for its publishing programs provided by the following agencies:
the Government of Canada, the Canada Council for the Arts and
the Province of British Columbia through the BC Arts Council
and the Book Publishing Tax Credit.

Cover artwork by Ella Collier and
Getty Images/aleksandarvelasevic
Edited by Tanya Trafford
Author photo by Rebecca Wellman

Printed and bound in Canada.

25 24 23 22 • 1 2 3 4

To Wilson's 5C Story Ninjas!

August, Lillian, Cole, Trinity, Emily, Erik, Alli,

Olivia, Annika, Saige, Zack, Joel, Heather,

Kiana, Tessa, Sam, Neil, Grayson, Brock,

Landyn (and, yes, for you too, Graham!)

All of you are rock stars. Thanks for

helping me with the story.

Chapter One

It was a warm October afternoon in the Yukon River valley. I stood on a beaver dam in the middle of a stream. This was my last stop of the day on the trapline.

I saw a beaver in the trap on the edge of the stream. It was not dead. It sat near a beaver house. One front leg was caught in the trap.

Something had gone wrong, I thought. The trap had a one-way slide on a cable. A trapped beaver always dove into the water to get away. The slide would let it go down, but not up again. It would drown.

Not this one.

Its front leg was probably broken. It must be in a lot of pain. I wondered how long the beaver had been in the trap.

"Just when I thought I could not hate trapping any more than I do."

There was nobody around to hear me. I walked this trapline, owned by my foster parents, alone. Talking to myself made it seem less lonely. Soon I would be sixteen. Then I would be old enough to leave. I would never again be forced to trap, kill and skin another animal.

I walked the rest of the way across the beaver dam. It was made of sticks and mud. It held back the water of a deep pond. A little stream ran over the top of it.

On the other side, I walked around the beaver house. It was also made of sticks and mud. It was round and high. It was almost the size of a small car. The only way into the beaver house was through a tunnel. One end of the tunnel was underwater. A beaver would swim into the tunnel. It would come up inside the house. The house was strong. Not even a grizzly bear could tear it apart.

Every time I saw a beaver house, I thought of this YouTube video I'd seen. A guy who did something that looked really crazy. And the beavers didn't attack him. And he survived.

I stepped toward the beaver. It flipped into the water when I got close. It slapped its broad tail and dove out of sight. It took the trap with it.

Beavers splash their tails to warn other beavers of danger.

How about that, I thought. The beaver could not escape the trap. But it still wanted to make sure others stayed clear.

I reached the edge of the water. I saw that the cable with the one-way slide had come loose from the post. That was why the beaver had not drowned. I watched bubbles pop up from the beaver underneath. It was at the edge of the chain that held the trap. It had nowhere to go. Soon it would run out of air. It would have to come to the surface again.

I also carried a rifle in case of a grizzly bear attack. I set down my backpack. I lifted the rifle. I waited.

The beaver came to the surface. All that showed was its nose and black eyes and the top of its head. It looked like it was too tired to move.

The best thing I could do for the beaver was kill it quickly. My foster father would yell at me if I put a hole in the beaver fur.

I would have to shoot it in the head. Then I would have to skin it like the other beavers I had trapped.

I aimed the rifle at the beaver. It stared at me.

I thought of how much pain the beaver had already suffered. I thought about how much I hated to work the trapline. I was not going to kill this beaver.

I set the safety device on the rifle so that it could not shoot. I rested the rifle against my backpack. I removed my jacket. I put the jacket down beside me.

I grabbed the chain to bring the beaver to shore. The beaver began to splash to try to get away. It was strong. I began to slide to the water as it pulled. I kicked over a big rock. I dug my boots into the ground. Now the beaver would not be able to pull me into the pond. But still it tried to get away.

It took five minutes for the beaver to tire. I pulled the chain again. The beaver wasn't fighting anymore.

I dragged the beaver onto the land. It was barely moving. I wrapped my jacket over the beaver so that it could not bite me. Then I opened the trap. The beaver's leg was broken. But the animal would live.

I unrolled my jacket and stepped back.

The beaver pushed away from the jacket. It looked at me one last time. It slid into the water. I watched bubbles rise as it swam under the water. More bubbles where it entered the tunnel under the water. Then nothing.

I leaned over to grab my jacket. I saw something in the dirt where I had kicked over the big rock.

It was a gold nugget the size of a baseball.

Chapter Two

I knew that people often found gold in the streams that led to the Yukon River. Where I lived was down the river from Dawson City. Gold was first found there over a hundred years ago. Once it had been a big city in the middle of the wilderness. Then the mines ran out of gold. Most of the people left. But tourists still came to pan for gold.

I picked up the nugget. I could barely close my fingers around it. I was surprised at how heavy it was. The surface was dull and dirty. I polished it with my sleeve. The gold became shinier.

I did not know how much it was worth. I did know that my foster parents would take it from me.

They would not be able to do that if I was sixteen. But then, if I was, I wouldn't be here. This find meant I had to speed up my plan to escape. I had to get to Dawson City. I would sell the gold there. I would put the money in a bank account. I would go south to a city like Vancouver. I would find work. I would live by myself. Freedom.

The nugget was so big that it wouldn't fit into the pocket of my jeans. If I put it into my jacket, though, Dan would probably see it. Dan Cork, my foster father.

But if I put it in my backpack, he would see it there for sure. He always emptied my pack to check the furs.

I wondered where I should hide it.

I thought about the trapline cabin. Most traplines in the Yukon went for hundreds of miles. Most had one or two cabins along the way for shelter during the winter.

But our cabin was too far back up the stream. I was supposed to meet my foster father at the river soon. I did not have time to go there and back.

If I buried the nugget, it might be a while before I came back to this stream. Any day now, it would snow. Then how would I be able to find it?

I thought about cutting a mark into a tree. I could bury it by the tree. I could even put it *in* the tree.

What if my foster father saw the mark? It probably wouldn't happen. But it could. That worried me.

What if there was a forest fire? It probably wouldn't happen. But it could. That worried me.

I realized something that struck me as funny. Not funny ha-ha. But funny strange. Finding this much gold had suddenly given me big worries.

Then I saw the solution. I smiled.

I would always be able to find the beaver house. It was the last one on the trapline. It was the one closest to the Yukon River.

I took a few steps and stopped at the sticks and mud of the beaver house. The house was as tall as I was. I pulled my knife out. I hacked a hole into the dried mud between some sticks. I pushed the nugget into the hole. I covered it with fresh mud from the shoreline. I washed the mud off my hands. I made knife marks on the sticks so I could find the exact spot later.

Now I was less worried. My foster father would never notice the marker. A forest fire would not burn the beaver house at the pond.

I closed my eyes and imagined what it would be like. To live on my own with lots of money in the bank.

Then I heard a rifle shot. And another one. There was a short silence. Then two more shots.

Chapter Three

The rifle shots meant that Dan had finished checking his traps. He always fired rifle shots because he did not like to wait long for me.

I followed the stream toward the Yukon River. I reached the last bend in the stream. The Yukon River in front of me was wide and fast. The river was lined with large spruce trees. Rocky hills on the other side seemed to push against the edge of the sky.

There were two canoes pulled up on the shore. Dan stood by the canoes. He was a big man. He had long dark hair. He had a big dark beard. His clothing was dirty and old. I was just as tall. I was not nearly as heavy. My hair was just as dark and just as long. But I did not have a beard. Not that I hadn't tried to grow one. And I kept my clothes clean.

"Your backpack better be full of furs," Dan said. "Let me see."

I slipped out of the backpack. I set it on the gravel on the shore. Dan opened it and pulled out the furs. They were sticky with blood.

"Not enough, Matt," Dan said. "This won't even pay for all the food you eat."

Dan always said that.

I kept my mouth shut. I knew my foster parents got lots of money to take care of me. It was the only reason they did it. When I was gone, they would get another young kid and more money. The kid would probably be around ten. Old enough to get lots of work out of him until he was sixteen. They would make that young kid learn how to do trapline work. He would wash all the dishes and do all the laundry. He would watch Dan's wife, Jill, drink vodka every night and fall asleep drunk.

That young kid would also learn never to talk back to Dan. Otherwise Dan would hit him. Like Dan had hit me.

Or maybe the kid would disappear. About ten years back, they'd had a foster kid who got lost working this trapline. People had searched for days. They'd used airplanes and helicopters. They'd never found him.

There was something scary about Dan. Sometimes at night I wondered if that foster kid really had been lost. Or if Dan had snapped on him. I hated being alone in the wilderness with Dan. As much as I hated trapping animals for him.

"Load your canoe," Dan said. "I don't have all day."

Dan sat on a log. He smoked a cigarette. He watched me do the work.

I put the furs into the backpack. I carefully tied it to the frame inside my canoe. If the canoe ever tipped over, the backpack would stay with it. If it tipped over, my job was to float with the canoe to bring it to shore.

When the snow came, we would come to the trapline by snowmobiles. I liked that better than traveling by canoe. Falling into the river would be dangerous. Not because I would drown. I always wore a life jacket. But the water was cold. I would need to find a way to build a fire to dry off. Otherwise there was a chance, at this time of year, of freezing to death. I always had waterproof matches in my pocket.

I finished tying the last knot. I put on my life jacket. I did not tell Dan I was ready. If I did, Dan would say, "What, you think I'm stupid? You think I can't tell when you are ready?"

Dan walked toward me. He threw his cigarette butt into the river. I hated seeing that.

"Scrape the propeller on rocks and I will scrape your hide," Dan said. "Each month you cost me enough as it is."

Dan put on his life jacket. He grabbed a paddle from his canoe. He pushed his canoe into the water. He hopped in as it began to float. He paddled into the middle of the river.

I did the same. At the back of the canoe was a small motor. It was tipped up so that it would not hit any rocks. I waited until the water was deep. I tipped the propeller into the water. I started the motor. I followed Dan down the river.

In two hours we would reach the cabin where Dan and Jill lived. I did not call the cabin a home. It did not feel like a home. It was only a place where I lived. It had a woodstove. In the winter, the cabin was always filled with furs that were stretched on frames to dry. It always smelled of cigarette smoke.

For a long time I had been looking forward to November 18. The day I turned sixteen.

But now I needed to find a way to get
out of here sooner. To get the gold into
Dawson City. Without Dan or Jill knowing
about it.

Chapter Four

Dawson City was a tiny place in a big wilderness. But it was the second-biggest city in the Yukon. Whitehorse, the biggest, was about a seven-hour drive away on gravel roads.

The Dawson City Library was in the Robert Service School. The school was named after a famous poet. He was also a bank teller. I did not go to that school. Dawson City was an hour's drive from our cabin. I was homeschooled. I got the books I needed from the library whenever we came to town.

Dan dropped me off at the library. He went to shop for food. Since we didn't come to town often, he had to buy a lot of food. That would give me time.

As soon as Dan drove off, I walked the other way from the library. I looked for rocks as I walked. I found one just about the right size.

It did not take long to reach a place that bought gold. After all, this was Dawson City. There was still gold to be found around here.

I walked up to the counter at the front of the office. A woman stood behind it. She wore jeans and a T-shirt. Her hair was gray and short.

"Hello," I said. "I am doing a report for school. Could I ask you a question?"

"You just did," she said. She did not smile.

I thought about that. "Could I ask two more questions?"

"You are smarter than you look," she said. "That leaves you one question. Ask."

I put the rock on the counter. I could barely fit my fingers around it. The rock, of course, was the size of the nugget I had found.

"You are so funny," she said. She still didn't smile. "We don't buy rocks."

"I know. But if a nugget was this big," I said, "how much would it be worth? I want to make sure my report is accurate."

Now she looked interested. "This is for a school report? Or maybe you know someone who found a nugget this big. If you did, I could buy it from you."

"A school report," I said.

"Why don't you do that tube thing?" she suggested. "Look for a video about it."

"YouTube," I said. "We don't have internet where I live."

"The library does," she said. "Why don't you look there? And if you ever find a nugget this big, then come see me."

"Thank you," I said. "But would you be able to tell me how much it might be worth?"

"I would say over a hundred thousand dollars."

"Do you pay right away? Do you need a bank account to transfer the money?"

"Are you sure this is for a school report? Your questions are quite specific."

"Yes," I said.

"It would not be smart for anyone to get paid that kind of money in cash. It would be better to put it into a bank account."

That helped. I needed to get a bank account here in Dawson City. Then there would be a place for the money. I could use a bank card to take out what I needed.

"Thank you," I said. "That will help with my report."

"Sure," she said. "Or maybe I will see you back here someday soon."

I walked out the door. I was worried. I could tell she had not believed my story about the school report.

I was even more worried after I got on the computer. She was right. The nugget was worth *a lot* of money.

Now I was even more afraid of losing it.

I thought it might be a good idea to write a report about gold. In case anyone asked. So I looked up some more facts and started putting them on paper. And that's what gave me an idea for the perfect hiding place.

Chapter Five

Two weeks later, in the middle of the day, I was at the trapline cabin. The sky had turned gray. Snow was starting to fall.

Dan was working a trapline on the other stream. He expected me to start a fire in the stove. He always wanted the cabin warm when he got there at the end of the day.

I had set up traps on the stream on the way here. After my break I would set more traps upstream. Then I would come back to the cabin and meet Dan. Tomorrow we would each go back to our streams to check all the traps we had set.

Traps of all sizes were hung on the outside walls of the cabin. I rested my rifle under some of those traps. I put my backpack on the ground beside a stack of firewood. The backpack was almost empty. The next day I would be using it to carry fur. From the animals killed in the traps I had set today.

I pulled the gold nugget out of my backpack. I had picked it up at the beaver house on my way. I stepped into the cabin.

The cabin was small. Bunk beds on one wall. A table and two chairs near the other wall. Shelves hung above the table with packages of food and cups and plates. Ropes of different sizes hung from hooks.

A wood-burning stove stood in the corner. Beside it was a propane torch for starting the fire. On top of the stove was a heavy iron frying pan for cooking.

I set the nugget on the kitchen table. I had a plan for hiding it until I could take it to Dawson City. First I needed to start a fire.

I walked outside to the pile of firewood. I grabbed two big pieces. I moved back to the doorway. I saw a mouse run across the floor inside. It ran toward the stove. It ran up the wall and onto the beam above the stove. Mice can climb nearly anything.

That's when I saw a small video camera on the beam. Just like the one Dan used at the house. It had a wide angle. It ran off a battery. It only shot video when there was movement. Dan would say he had set it up in case someone tried to steal something from the house.

But I knew better.

It had been a mistake to ask about a gold nugget in Dawson City. Somehow Dan had found out.

The big gold nugget was on the kitchen table. Where Dan would see it on the video. If I got rid of the camera, Dan would not know about the gold. But he would know I knew about the camera. He would ask what I had to hide.

When Dan looked at the video, would he see that I had noticed the camera? Maybe not. The daylight had been behind me when I was in the doorway. The brightness would make my face too dark.

It seemed smart to pretend I did not know about the camera. So I shut the door like everything was normal.

I put the wood into the stove. I started the propane torch. I touched the hot blue flame against the wood until it caught fire.

This was why Dan had the torch. On cold winter days it was nice to be able to get a fire going fast.

I thought more about what Dan would see on the video. How could I hide the nugget now?

I looked around the cabin. There was a coffee pot on the shelf. Perfect.

I grabbed the coffeepot to fill it with water from the stream. On my way outside, I picked up the gold nugget from the table. I put it inside the front of my shirt. I knew all of this would be on video for Dan to see.

I reached the stream. Snow was starting to stick to the ground. Already I was leaving footprints. Winter was here. Soon the streams and ponds would be covered in ice.

I thought about how the camera was pointed down into the cabin. It had a view of nearly all of the inside. The only place hidden from the camera was the stove directly below it. And the torch. And the frying pan.

That was lucky. I had planned to use the torch and frying pan to help me hide my gold.

I dropped the nugget into the coffeepot. I filled the rest of the pot with water from the stream. Back at the cabin I pulled my flashlight from my backpack. I put it into my back pocket. It would be hidden from the camera. So would the nugget in the coffee pot.

I walked inside and to the area where I would not be seen on camera.

I put the coffeepot onto the stove. I pulled the nugget out of the coffeepot. I put the nugget into the frying pan. I pulled the flashlight from my pocket. Now I could hide the nugget the way I had planned.

By the time I was finished, the coffee was ready.

I went outside and put my flashlight into the backpack. I went back inside and poured a cup of coffee. I sat at the kitchen table. I sipped the coffee and I thought some more.

I had decided to hide the gold until my birthday. That seemed the safest plan. But then I'd spotted the camera. Now I knew I would have to run away before Dan got to the cabin. I would walk along the stream to the Yukon River. I would paddle my canoe all the way down the river to Dawson City. It would be dark by then, but I would be safe. Even if I had to sleep in a doorway somewhere.

But then Dan pushed open the cabin door.

Chapter Six

Dan stepped into the cabin with his backpack and rifle. He also had my rifle. The snow on his jacket began to melt.

He set the backpack against the wall. He leaned both rifles beside it. He hung his jacket on a hook.

"Don't you have more traps to set upstream?" he asked.

"It doesn't take long to have a coffee when I start the fire for you," I said. "I always get my traps done."

I didn't ask why he was here. I didn't want the answer. All I needed was a chance to run before he saw the video.

Dan grabbed a coffee cup. He went to the stove. He poured coffee. He sat at the table, across from me.

The cabin was warm from the fire in the stove. But that wasn't why I felt sweat under my shirt. I wondered if he had been spying on me from outside the cabin somewhere.

"Not much left in the pot," Dan said as he sipped from his cup. "So you wasted time drinking two or three cups?"

He looked at me. Like he was a cat. And I was a mouse.

I thought of how the nugget in the pot had meant less space for water.

"I always get my traps done by the end of the day," I repeated.

"We can make another pot," Dan said. "How about you get some water and then chop some firewood?"

We didn't need firewood. Dan just wanted me outside and busy so he could check the video. When he saw the nugget, I was in trouble. He was a mean man. I thought of the foster kid who had disappeared ten years earlier.

I needed to run. Now.

But Dan was smart. If he didn't hear me chopping wood, he would know I had run. He could follow my footprints in the snow. It wouldn't take long for him to catch up to me. He had both rifles.

I had to think of something. But I also had to pretend I didn't know about the camera.

I went to the stove. I took the pot. I put on my coat. I walked to the door. "Back with water soon."

"Are you lazy or just stupid?" he asked.

"What?" I asked.

"I always tell you to take your rifle, no matter how short the trip. What if you ran into a grizzly?"

Surprised, I took my rifle. I went to the stream and filled the pot. The snow was falling hard. When I came back, Dan was standing in the doorway. By then I knew what to do.

"Happy to chop some wood," I said. "A visit to the outhouse first. That coffee ran right through me."

As soon as he closed the door, I would grab my flashlight from my backpack. I would go to the outhouse. I would make a big circle around the cabin until I reached the stream. Then I would run. Dan would wait and wait until he realized I had not gone to the outhouse. All I needed was ten minutes for a head start. As long as I got to my canoe on the Yukon River ahead of Dan.

Dan pulled out a pack of cigarettes. He lit one. He stood in the doorway and watched me as he smoked. Like he was watching for me to try to take something from the backpack. Like he was going to pounce anytime. Mind games.

I had no choice. I kept my rifle but left the backpack behind. Maybe I should just run now and leave everything behind. No, I would never make it. I would have to think of a new plan.

I walked to the far outside corner of the cabin. I turned to take the short trail through the trees to the outhouse.

I thought about what would happen when Dan saw the video. And what he might do to me if he caught me running away.

Dan had taught me many lessons about setting traps. The first lesson was to pretend you were the animal you wanted to trap. Dan had guessed what I might do. So he had set a trap with the camera.

Now I needed to guess what he would do. And set my own trap for him.

Chapter Seven

I returned to the cabin after my trip to the outhouse. Dan was still standing in the open doorway.

All the stuff from my backpack was on the ground. A blanket. My flashlight. My lunch bag. Trail mix. A small plastic box with things for in case I got lost. The box had fishing hooks and fishing line. Extra waterproof matches.

"Good thing you didn't meet a grizzly," Dan said. "Because I emptied your rifle when I first got to the cabin. Just in case I was right about your gold nugget. If I was wrong, it was still smart to remind you to take your rifle to the stream."

"Gold nugget?" I said. "I don't understand."

"Leave your rifle out here," Dan said. "Step inside."

"What is going on?" I asked. But I knew what was going on. I had guessed right. While I was gone, Dan had watched the video. He saw the gold nugget on the kitchen table. He saw me put it into my shirt. He saw me walk outside with it again. He thought I had put it in the backpack. He had not found it there.

"Step inside," Dan repeated. Snow blew past him into the cabin. He didn't seem to care.

"You wanted me to chop wood," I said.

Dan stepped away from the door. He came back with his rifle. He pointed it at me.

"Step inside," he said.

I did. He had moved a chair under the beam in the middle of the cabin. A long piece of rope was slung over the beam. The ends hung down on each side. There was a noose at one end of the rope.

A noose! Would he really do that?

I stopped. Dan poked my back with the end of the rifle.

"Stand in front of the chair," Dan said. "Lift your hands and put them through the noose."

"Dan, this is crazy," I said. "What is going on?"

He poked me again. "Hands through the noose. Or I drop it around your neck."

I stood in front of the chair. I lifted my hands and put them through the noose.

Dan pulled on the other end of the rope until my hands were high above my head. The noose grew tight around my wrists. He pulled so hard that I had to stand on my tiptoes.

Holding the rope with one hand, he set down his rifle. He stepped onto the chair. He tied the other end of the rope to the noose around my wrists.

He stepped off the chair and moved it in front of me.

He grabbed the propane torch and sat down on the chair. He lit the torch. He smiled at the hot blue flame.

"Where is it?" he asked.

"Where is what?" I said.

"You asked a gold buyer in Dawson City about selling a gold nugget," he said. "One as big as a baseball. Where is it?"

"I was writing a school report," I said. "It is on my desk at the house."

"I read it," he said. "And I looked all through your bedroom for a real nugget. Because I thought there was a good chance you did find one. Maybe too big to put in your pocket. Maybe too big to put in your backpack. Plus I empty out your pack when I take the furs. So I thought maybe it was still on the trapline somewhere."

My only chance was to pretend I did not know about the camera.

"You're not making sense," I said. "All I did was write a school report."

Dan pointed the torch at me. The flame hissed. "I asked myself what I would do if I were you. I would leave it somewhere on the trapline. Maybe even hide it in the cabin. Then I would get it on our next trip here.

And run away with it when foster dad was working the other trapline. Was I right?"

My arms hurt. I couldn't move and I was barely able to stand.

"It was just a school report," I said.

He walked to the shelf and came back with the small video camera. "I ran ahead of you this morning. I hid a camera in the cabin. I have video that shows the nugget. It also shows you taking it outside."

"What?" I said.

He smiled. "You are easier to trap than a beaver. You have a choice. If you tell me now, I won't have to use the torch to burn you. If there are no burn marks on your skin, it will be your word against mine. People will believe me. Not you. It means I can take the nugget and let you live and let you come back with me."

He stood up from the chair and moved closer. He held the torch so close to my face that I could feel heat from the flame.

"But if I have to burn you," he said, "people might believe you. That means I wouldn't be able to let you live. I would go back to Dawson City and tell everyone you were lost. We would send out airplanes to search for you. But no one would ever find your body."

"Dan!"

"Your choice. Tell me where it is and live. Or make me burn you until you tell me, and then you die."

I stared at him. He stared back.

"Okay," I said. "I had it hidden inside my shirt when you walked into the cabin. At the outhouse, I hid it under the roof. Where we keep the toilet-paper rolls."

He turned off the torch. "If it's not there, I won't give you a choice when I get back. I will burn small holes in you until you tell me where it really is."

He grabbed his rifle and walked out into the blowing snow.

Chapter Eight

I stood there on tiptoes below the beam, alone in the cabin. I thought of how Dan had climbed onto the chair to wrap the rope around the noose.

To escape, I needed to be able to stand on the chair too.

I lifted my feet and let my body hang

by my wrists. The knots in the noose hurt against my skin. But not as much as burn marks from a propane torch would if Dan came back.

Was it too soon to hope to hear Dan scream?

That didn't matter as much as trying to escape. I swung my body backward.

Then forward. Toward the chair where Dan had been sitting.

Backward again.

Forward again.

Finally I was able to hook the top part of the chair with my foot. My body weight pulled the chair toward me.

I swung again. This time it was easier

to hook the chair with my foot. I pulled it closer. And closer.

Then I was able to stand on the chair. I kept waiting to hear Dan scream from the path to the outhouse.

Nothing.

I lowered my hands to my face. I moved my wrists toward my mouth.

I bit into the side of the big knot that made the noose. I pulled hard with my teeth. The knot only loosened a little.

I took a breath. I still kept hoping I would hear Dan scream.

Still nothing.

I pulled again at the knot with my teeth. And again. Finally it slipped loose. I yanked at the rope. It fell from the beam. My hands were free.

I did not feel free. What if Dan returned right now?

I grabbed my coat. I pushed open the door. I was afraid I might see Dan walking around the corner. His rifle in his hand. He wasn't there. But I did not hear any screaming either.

I took what I needed most from the ground near my backpack. The flashlight. And the survival kit with matches and fish hooks and fishing line.

I did not grab my rifle. Dan had the bullets.

I wanted to run as fast as I could toward the Yukon River.

But I needed to know if I had enough time to get ahead of Dan.

So I walked the other way. Around the cabin and toward the outhouse. Past the traps hanging on the outside wall.

One trap was no longer there. A huge bear trap. Just in case I had guessed right about what Dan might do once he saw the video. Because Dan had taught me well. All you needed was the right bait and a trap in the right place.

A gold nugget the size of a baseball was the right bait. Especially because Dan didn't know that I had seen the hidden camera.

But had I picked the right place? I really needed to know. Otherwise, Dan would be right behind me as I tried to escape to the river.

Dan had also told me that a trapped animal is a dangerous animal.

I did not go up the path to make sure that he had been caught in the trap.

I went in a wide circle to come up behind the outhouse. It took me five minutes, going slowly and carefully. I was glad for the snow. My footsteps made no sound. It was not easy to see very far. If I couldn't see far, Dan couldn't see far.

At the back of the outhouse, I got onto my belly. I did not want to make it easy for Dan to shoot at me.

During the summer, a tree had fallen across the path on the other side. Dan had made me chop off all the branches to make it easy to step over it. There was really only one place for the front foot to land on the other side. That's where I had set the bear trap wide open. I had covered it with leaves. The falling snow had made it even harder to see. And I had looped the chain around the base of another tree. I didn't want him pulling it loose.

Had I chosen the right place to go with the right bait?

I peeked around the corner.

I saw Dan, his face low to the ground like mine was. He had his rifle resting on a fallen tree. Aimed the other way. He was waiting to shoot me when I came up the path to see if my trap had worked.

Yes, I had chosen the right place. I could see that the bottom of his right leg was stuck in the huge bear trap. He should have been screaming in pain. Instead he was trying to trap me. Again.

I did not feel bad for him. Not after he had promised to burn me. Not when he was waiting there to shoot me.

When he decided I wasn't coming up the path, he would take the trap off his leg. It was a lot of work, but it was possible. I could only hope his leg was too injured for him to chase me. Or if it wasn't, that my head start would be enough. All I needed was to get to the canoes ahead of him.

I backed away from the outhouse. Time to run.

Chapter Nine

It was still snowing when I reached the bank of the Yukon River an hour later. And it was getting dark. I did not care. Once I was in my canoe, I would be free. When I reached Dan and Jill's house, I would sneak inside to grab a sleeping bag and some ID. Jill wouldn't hear me. She would be drunk and asleep. With dirty dishes in the sink.

I was surprised to see a long chain on the ground beside the canoes. With a lock that was open.

Of course. Dan had expected me to run away. He would have chained and locked the canoes to a tree so that I couldn't take one.

That made sense. What didn't make sense was why they were no longer chained.

I had a bad thought. A really bad thought. The only person who could unlock the chain was the person who had locked it. Dan.

I turned to run back up the stream. Too late. Dan stepped out of the trees. He pointed his rifle at me.

"Bad luck for you that the bear trap didn't break my leg," he said. "Bad luck for you that I knew how to get here on a straight line and beat you here. Let me see you empty your pockets. All of them."

"I don't have it," I said. "I wondered if you might get here first. So I hid it."

"Empty your pockets."

I could see the anger and hatred on his face. It would be too easy for him to hide my body. Then take his canoe to Dawson City and call for a search party that would never find me.

All I had was my flashlight and the survival kit. I pulled each out of a pocket. I showed him my other pockets. As I did this, I tried to think of a way to escape.

I thought of the beaver house up the stream. I thought of that YouTube video. I had nothing to lose. If I didn't try, I was dead.

"I told you," I said. "The gold is a short way upstream. Will you let me live if I give it to you?"

"Of course," he said.

I knew he was lying.

"Follow me," I said. I put the flashlight and survival kit back in my pockets.

It did not take long for us to reach the beaver house where I had first found the nugget. I was very afraid of what I had to do next. But I had to try. It was my only chance to live.

"I cut a hole in the mud of this beaver house," I told Dan. "I cut into some sticks to mark the spot. See?"

As he turned to look, I dove into the deep dark water. Just like the guy had done in that video.

The water was cold. I swam underwater toward the spot where I remembered seeing bubbles. Where the beaver that I had let go had gone into the tunnel.

I felt around with my hands.

I was almost out of air when I found it. The edge of a large hole. It had to be the tunnel.

Now I had to choose. Go up for air and let Dan shoot at me. Or push forward and hope I did not get stuck in the tunnel and drown.

One way I would die for sure.

The other way, maybe not. The guy on the video had made it. And even filmed himself from inside the beaver house.

I pushed forward. The tunnel was wide. I did not get stuck. I made it out of the tunnel and inside the beaver house.

I took a deep breath. It was smelly.

It was also very dark. I heard some chirping sounds.

I wondered if I should just stay where I was. With my body in the water of the tunnel. And my head sticking up for air.

But the water was too cold.

I crawled forward. It was warm. Of course it was. The heat from the beavers would make it warm.

I waited for one of them to attack me in the dark. Instead I heard more chirping.

I reached up. I was surprised at how big the den was. I could sit without hitting my head on the roof.

I needed light. I knew my flashlight would not work.

I pulled my survival kit out of my pocket. There were at least twenty matches. Enough to take a quick look around.

I lit a match. The flame showed me that the space here was bigger than the inside of a car. I saw five beavers against the other wall. They were different sizes. They stared at me. I stared at them.

One of the beavers was very large.

"Hey, buddy," I said. "Nice to see you again."

Strange. Saving his life had saved mine. Even if Dan had an ax, no way could he chop through the roof and reach me.

All he could do was wait for me to come out.

Chapter Ten

"Do you have another rock for me?" the gold buyer asked.

For an answer I put my flashlight on the counter.

"You are just as funny as last time," she said. "We don't buy flashlights either."

She sniffed. "What isn't funny is how

bad you smell. And you look horrible. Were you up all night using this flashlight?"

She probably would not believe my true answer. I had waited in the beaver house until I was sure it was dark outside. I had taken a deep breath and gone back down the tunnel. I had swum underwater as far as I could. I had come up for air a long way away. The falling snow had made it impossible for Dan to see me.

I had pulled myself out of the water at the far edge of the pond. I had walked a big circle, knowing that Dan would be waiting at the beaver house. I had pushed a canoe into the river. I was cold, but the dry life jacket had helped. I had known I would be okay for the half hour it would take to reach Dan's cabin. I had stopped there for a sleeping bag and ID. Jill was passed out and didn't notice me. I had gotten back in the canoe, wrapped myself in the sleeping bag and paddled downriver to Dawson City.

When I got to Dawson City, I'd slept in that sleeping bag for the rest of the night. As soon as the bank was open, I had opened an account.

Now I was here. With a flashlight on the counter. I put my ID on the counter too.

This unsmiling woman had already blabbed about a kid who might have found a giant nugget. If Dan reported I was missing along the trapline, she would hear about it right away. The news would have my name. She would remember me. She would tell the police Matt McEwan had been in town. It would stop anyone from sending out a search party. By then I would be long gone. It would be easy to get a ride south on the Klondike Highway. I would be in Whitehorse by dark tonight. Where Dan would have no chance of finding me.

I unscrewed the flashlight.

"We don't buy used flashlight batteries either," she said.

"I bet you use a propane torch to melt gold," I said.

"Yes," she said. "Everyone who handles gold does."

"How about we melt the gold inside the flashlight?"

It would not take long. I knew because it had not taken long to melt the gold in the frying pan. And then pour it into the flashlight handle.

"Wow," she said. "You must have been really worried that someone would steal it from you."

I smiled. "You have no idea."

Author's Note

Is it possible to swim into a beaver house? While doing my research for *Trapped*, I found a video on YouTube titled "What's Inside a Beaver Home?" That led me to another video, "Swimming Underwater into a Beaver Lodge." Both videos strongly warn not to try this yourself. So the short answer is yes, it is possible.

But I must repeat that warning: DO NOT TRY IT!!

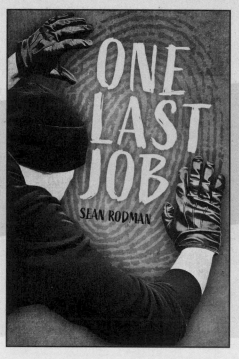

Chapter One

The robbery happens fast. We never even see it coming.

Gramps and I are sitting on his old green couch. We are watching TV. Taking turns answering the questions that the game-show host asks. I am almost always right. Particularly anything to do with sports or geography. When the show finishes, Gramps turns to me.

"When did you get so smart?" he says. "You act like some dumb tough guy around your friends, Mikey. I swear that big brain of yours is going to take you—"

There is a crash of glass from the back door near the kitchen. I stand up, my plate clattering to the floor.

Then the burglar is right in front of us. His face is completely hidden. A red bandanna over his mouth. Mirrored sunglasses across his eyes. A black Yankees ball cap pulled down low on his head.

He holds a dull gray pistol in one hand and levels it at my chest. Then jerks it toward Gramps. Then back to me. I slowly put up my hands and ease back down onto the couch.

My heartbeat thuds in my ears. I can feel my chest tighten. This kind of stuff happens in our neighborhood occasionally. It never ends well.

Gramps has a heart condition too. Something like this could trigger an attack. My mom told me that I have to give him pills if that happens. But I've never actually done it.

The burglar shouts something through the red bandanna covering his mouth. I can't tell what he is saying. Neither can Gramps.

"I'm sorry," says Gramps politely. "You'll have to repeat that."

I tear my eyes away from the gun to look at Gramps. How can he be so calm? Gramps blinks slowly behind his thick glasses. He coughs softly.

The burglar turns his head a little to the side. He's a skinny guy. For a second he looks like a weird bird with his head like that. Gramps clears his throat and tries again.

"I can't understand you. Look, I guess it's my fault. I'm not wearing my hearing aids. But that rag over your mouth? It isn't helping. Maybe if you take it off?"

The burglar pauses. Thinks about it. Frustrated, he rips off the bandanna.

"This is a robbery!" he shouts again. Louder. Angrier. "Do not move a freakin' muscle!" He points with his gun for emphasis.

"That I understand," says Gramps. "And I won't move. It takes me half an hour to get up from this couch. You've got nothing to worry about."

Still, the burglar pulls out a couple of thick black plastic zip ties. Using them, he ties up Gramps and then me. The little plastic zip ties aren't enough to stop us. But they are enough to slow us down long enough for him to shoot us. If we are dumb enough to move. While he's tying us up, I study his face. He has a little cold sore on the edge of his lip. His breath smells like garlic.

Satisfied, the burglar stuffs the gun into the waistband of his jeans. Then he starts to search the one-room apartment. It won't take him long. The place is tiny. A single bed with a dresser next to it. A mini-kitchen with a mini-fridge. A desk. And a green couch, where we sit. All tied up.

The burglar pulls out a drawer from my grandpa's desk. He shakes it upside down. Papers and pens fall to the floor.

"You want some pencils?" says Gramps. "I've even got pens, if that's what you're looking for."

"Don't make him mad," I hiss at Gramps. The burglar ignores us and keeps on making a mess. He dumps a bunch of files out, papers flying everywhere. Then sweeps a stack of hardcover books from their shelves. He empties kitchen cabinets. Pots and pans clatter across the linoleum.

"He's not very good at this," says Gramps.

"Shut it!" roars the burglar, not looking at us. He's busy tossing clothes out of the dresser onto the floor.

Gramps lowers his voice and leans toward me. "Seriously, this guy is an amateur. And I should know."

Gramps has lived, as he puts it, an "adventurous life." He doesn't talk much about it, and neither do my parents. But I know he had a criminal career that ended with a couple of years in prison.

"How about I save us all some time?" says Gramps to the burglar. "There's twenty bucks in a pickle jar by the door. It's for the cleaning lady. Aside from that, you're not going to find anything here. I've got nothing to hide."

Sigmund Brouwer is the award-winning author of over 100 books for young readers. He has won the Christy Book of the Year and an Arthur Ellis Award, and has been nominated for two TD Children's Literature Awards and the Red Maple Award. For years, Sigmund has captivated students with his Rock & Roll Literacy Show and Story Ninja program during his school visits, reaching up to eighty thousand students per year. Sigmund lives in Red Deer, Alberta.

For more information on all the books

in the Orca Anchor line, please visit

orcabook.com